WRITTEN BY
J.E. BRIGHT

ILLUSTRATED BY
TIM LEVINS

SUPERMAN CREATED BY
JERRY SIEGEL AND
JOE SHUSTER
BY SPECIAL ARRANGEMENT WITH

RAINTREE IS AN IMPRINT OF CAPSTONE GLOBAL LIBRARY
LIMITED, A COMPANY INCORPORATED IN ENGLAND AND
WALES HAVING ITS REGISTERED OFFICE AT 264 BANBURY
ROAD, OXFORD, OX2 7DY - REGISTERED COMPANY
NUMBER: 6695582

WWW.RAINTREE.CO.UK
MYORDERS@RAINTREE.CO.UK

APPLICATIONS FOR THE COPYRIGHT OWNER'S WRITTEN
PERMISSION SHOULD BE ADDRESSED TO THE PUBLISHER.

ART DIRECTOR: BOB LENTZ AND BRANN GARVEY
DESIGNER: HILARY WACHOLZ

ISBN 978 1 4747 3283 3
21 20 19 18 17
10 9 8 7 6 5 4 3 2 1

BRITISH LIBRARY CATALOGUING IN PUBLICATION DATA
A FULL CATALOGUE RECORD FOR THIS BOOK IS AVAILABLE
FROM THE BRITISH LIBRARY.

PRINTED AND BOUND IN CHINA

CONTENTS

CHAPTER 1
SUNLIGHT 6

CHAPTER 2
PARANORMAL...................................18

CHAPTER 3
EVOLUTION 32

CHAPTER 4
GHOST IN THE MACHINE 48

CHAPTER 5
CYBORG SUPERMAN 62

Years ago, in a distant galaxy, the planet Krypton exploded. Its only survivor was a baby called Kal-El who escaped in a rocket ship. After landing on Earth, he was adopted by the Kents, a kind couple who named him Clark. The boy soon discovered he had extraordinary abilities fuelled by the yellow sun of Earth. He chose to use these powers to help others, and so he became Superman - the guardian of his new home.

He is...

CHAPTER 1

SUNLIGHT

Dr Hank Henshaw gritted his teeth. He and his crew were starting re-entry into Earth's atmosphere in the space shuttle *Excalibur*, and already powerful gravitational forces were pressing down on him. The shift back to gravity after being weightless for a few days in space made Hank feel like he was slowly being crushed in a giant, invisible fist.

Hank felt proud about the mission they'd accomplished. It had been a complete success.

Hank and his crew had flown *Excalibur* outside of Earth's atmosphere, past the magnetic field encircling the planet. They soared into space and into the solar winds to collect cosmic rays that were so high-frequency nobody had even proven their existence.

Until now. Hank had found proof. Not only had he identified the cosmic rays, he'd managed to collect and store some.

But he hadn't done it alone. Without his wife, Terri, who had invented the crystal storage container for the mysterious radiation, he would never have been able to prove his theories were true. Yes, he'd invented the detector, but the two of them were an unstoppable team. Hank smiled slowly as the g-forces pulled at his face.

Hank thought about the opportunities that would open up after this. The resources and money. The power he would have.

"Buckle up, everyone," barked Steven Bishop, the commander of the *Excalibur*.

"It's getting rougher all the way down," said the pilot, James Dobbins. "And we're getting heavier."

"Think light thoughts," added Commander Steve.

Hank leaned into his shoulder harness, striving to breathe calmly as he was shaken around in his seat. They were in the outer atmosphere, passing through the thermosphere towards the mesosphere. The g-forces and the shaking were going to get much worse before the shuttle reached the stratosphere below.

Hank owed a debt of gratitude to the shuttle's crew, Steve and Jim. They were like super heroes, flying off the planet into outer space. The journey on the *Excalibur* had been the trip of a lifetime, and Hank was sad that it was almost over.

Terri waved her hand, and they turned to look at one another through their helmets. Hank could only faintly see his wife's eyes. "Are you okay?" she asked.

Hank smiled. "Never better," he replied. "And you're here, which makes it perfect."

It *was* perfect. They had accomplished a scientific breakthrough, something that would be listed in science books forever.

Sailing down through the freezing, bumpy mesosphere, Hank caught sight of a flare of light through the cockpit window.

Shielding his eyes with his hand, Hank turned as far as his suit allowed him to look. A glowing arc of molten material spewed out of the Sun like a tentacle.

"Solar flare," Hank whispered in awe. He raised his voice. "Hey, it's a solar flare!"

They'd expected that the Sun would be quiet for the duration of their mission, but the Sun was unpredictable. Now, a solar flare sprayed cosmic rays and radiation everywhere, which was extremely dangerous for the astronauts.

"I see it," Steve said grimly.

"What does it mean?" Terri demanded. "Is –" She broke off as the solar flare thickened and looped. It glowed even brighter now, nearly doubling in size.

Hank gasped.

A solar explosion of that magnitude could fry communication satellites and disrupt the electrical grid. Earth's ionosphere would protect the world from the radiation, but Hank and *Excalibur* had just entered the magnetic field that shielded the planet. They were still at the weak outer edge. The flare could fry the shuttle – along with the astronauts inside!

"Roll starboard!" Steve ordered.

"Commander," Jim replied, "if we raise our tiles, we'll get too hot!"

Hank gripped the hand rests on his seat. The tiles on the bottom of the shuttle were a special ceramic that prevented the craft from burning up on re-entry. Steve obviously thought the tiles might protect them from the solar radiation, too.

"We have time for re-entry," Steve said. "But that radiation will cook us from the inside out. Roll –!"

Suddenly, the window blazed with bright orange light. Steve screamed. Hank, Terri and Jim cried out, too. The radiation from the solar flare hit them head-on.

Hotter than fire, Hank thought as his body was wracked with agony. Scorching light filled the cockpit. The light was so bright that Hank felt it warming his eyes through his eyelids. The radiation sank into his skin, making him itch like crazy.

Jim rolled *Excalibur* enough to put the cockpit in the shadow of the tilted wing, protecting them from the worst of the solar flare. They barely avoided being burned alive inside their spacesuits.

Although, Hank wasn't sure they'd survive the radiation they had already suffered. *Where's Superman when you need him?* Hank thought.

"Hank?" Terri moaned. "I feel . . . strange."

"Me, too," he told her, gasping. "Stay strong, Terri –"

"I can't hold it," said Jim, his voice cracking. The shuttle shimmied violently. "Our re-entry is getting too hot!"

"Roll back portside," Steve said. "The worst of the flare must have passed."

"We don't have a choice," Jim replied. "We have to straighten out, or the ship will be torn apart on re-entry."

As Jim lowered the right wing, the solar flare blasted into the cockpit again.

CRACKLE! CRACKLE! The radiation wasn't as hot now that the solar wave had passed, but the crew of *Excalibur* still felt its blistering heat.

With the shuttle straightened, the craft stopped jittering as badly. But the damage had been done. Flashing orange warning lights and red danger lights lit up across the control panels.

Hank closed his eyes. Under his spacesuit, his skin felt like it was suffering from very bad sunburn. His headache was agonizing. He felt his body was being rearranged at a molecular level.

Even if he survived, Hank would be suffering from severe radiation sickness. There was no avoiding it. *Like Marie Curie*, Hank thought. *She died researching radium.*

Hank wondered if his achievements, and his sacrifice, would bring him a Nobel Prize like it had for Curie.

Hank was lost in thought as the shuttle plunged towards Earth. *Excalibur* reached the thicker stratosphere, and the planet's magnetic field and ozone layer provided protection from the solar rays.

Hank opened his eyes to see that a bright light was coming from him. Hank pulled off a glove. His fingers shined from the inside. For a heart-stopping second, he saw his bones glowing inside his hand!

He glanced at Terri. Behind her mask, she was terrified. Her face flickered with bright red light, and her skin looked transparent, as though she was made of nothing but light.

CHAPTER 2

PARANORMAL

A loud pop sounded from the dashboard. **_FZZZZZZZZT!_** Sparks shot across the control panel.

"We're shorting out!" Steve cried. "Systems failing. No communication with Mission Control. We need to get this bird down alone."

"We're dropping like a rock," cried Jim. "Prepare for a hard landing . . . if we can even call it a landing."

Excalibur wobbled, then spun. Hank's stomach flipped over.

The view shifted jerkily from blue sky to brown landscape and back again. Seeing the ground spinning made Hank dizzy.

"We're on backup computer navigation," Jim warned. "We need to stabilize."

"I'm re-routing power to the thrusters and navigation system," said Steve. "It's going to get dark in here, but we might still have a chance of landing."

"Where?" Jim asked. "We're a thousand miles off course, in the middle of nowhere. We'll never get to a safe landing site!"

"Landing Site C," replied Steve, his breathing harsh. "It's our . . . only shot."

Hank closed his eyes again, listening to the astronauts. They were trained to keep calm in emergencies.

But Hank heard the stress in the astronauts' voices. Without communication with the ground support crews, they were flying blind. Landing Site C hosted shuttle training missions, but might not be prepared for a crash landing – especially as communications were down.

Excalibur straightened as the backup computer aligned the thrusters. Underneath the shuttle was an empty stretch of white desert, ringed by jagged orange rock formations in the distance.

"We're going to overshoot the sand," said Steve. His skin glowed with purplish-blue radioactive light. "I . . . ," he began. "I feel really tired."

"Commander!" Jim barked, as Steve slumped over in his seat.

Terri leaned forward against her restraints, her face glowing like Steve's, but red instead of purple and blue. "Jim, can you bring us down?" she asked. "Without Steve's help?"

"I can try," Jim replied. He grabbed the control stick firmly despite his twitching muscles. "I'll have to land her manually. The computer systems are too damaged."

CLICK! Jim pressed a button that turned off the backup computer control system. The orbiter shuddered in the air again.

Hank got shaken badly until Jim adjusted the rudder to help them drop more smoothly. Bits of metal and screws broke loose, and Hank watched with wide eyes as the metal flew towards Jim and stuck to him!

There was a gear stuck to the back of Jim's helmet, and chunks of a cabinet door stuck to his shoulder.

With the rocky desert rushing up at the shuttle, Hank didn't have time to think about the metal bits sticking to Jim. He gripped his hand rests as Jim steered them around tall stone formations, tilting the orbiter to fit under a huge rock arch. Up ahead was a cliff's edge.

"Hang on!" Jim yelled. "This is going to be rough!"

RUMMMMMMMMMBLE!

The orbiter jolted as the landing gear deployed. Hank bounced back in his seat as Jim let out the drag chute behind them. But they were still going so fast. They soared closer to the cliff's edge with every second that passed.

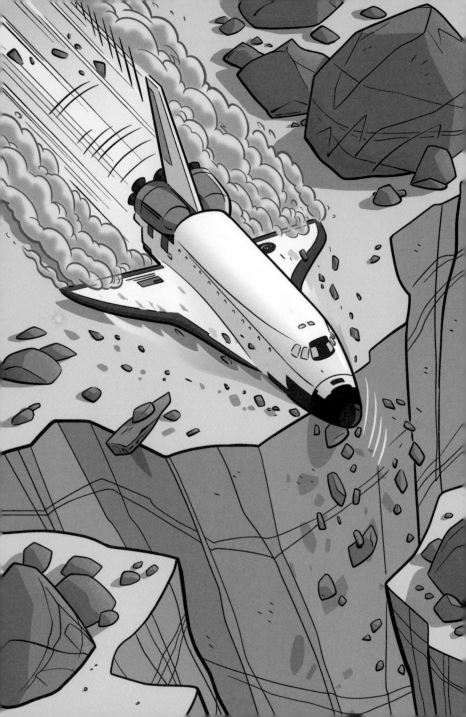

KIRRRRSH!

The orbiter skidded, careering towards the edge. Hank expected to be plummeting to his death by now. Instead, the shuttle slid to a stop.

Blue sky filled the cockpit view. The shuttle had stopped just centimetres from the edge of the cliff.

They had made it back to Earth alive.

Jim was unconscious. More chunks of metal were stuck all over him, clinging to his spacesuit.

Every molecule in Hank's body ached, but he unclasped his restraint harness and struggled to stand. He knew they weren't safe in the spaceship. "Help me," he gasped to Terri. "We need to get them out."

Her face flickering with red light, Terri freed herself from her seat. She grabbed Steve, who was glowing a sickly light blue, and pulled him towards the cockpit's emergency exit. Terri kicked open the hatch and yanked Steve outside.

Before he followed her, Hank rushed to the back of the ship and opened a storage locker. Inside was a silver canister that contained a sample of the radiation Hank had discovered.

A plume of smoke puffed out of the control panel, along with tongues of flame.

There wasn't time to get the big canisters down on the mid-deck, but there was no way Hank would leave without taking the sample. One day that radiation might be called Henshaw rays – named after him. He'd rather die than leave it behind.

Once he had the small canister tucked under his arm, Hank lugged Jim outside. Terri was resting a few steps away from the shuttle.

"Get far away!" Hank shouted. "It's going to explode!"

Terri dragged Steve towards a pile of boulders. Hank helped Jim to follow her, noticing with alarm that hunks of rock were sticking to Jim's body along with slivers of metal.

Dark, thick spirals of smoke issued from the shuttle. Hank and Terri laid the commander and pilot down on the sand behind the boulders.

Excalibur detonated in a blazing fireball. Flames shot around the boulders, and hunks of debris flew everywhere.

Terri and Hank ducked their heads over Jim and Steve. The heat was bad, but not as unbearable as the solar flare.

When the explosion died down, Hank grabbed Terri in a hug. "We made it," he said. He pulled off his helmet.

Terri took off her helmet, too, and stared at him. "Your hair's white!" she cried.

Hank smiled. Terri looked like she had a bad case of sunburn. Her face was lobster red. "You look sunburned," he said, "but otherwise okay."

"I'm fine," Terri agreed. She glanced at Steve and Jim. "But they're not. We have to get them out of the desert."

Steve glowed hot with blue radiation, and his eyes were discs of purple flame. Rocks and metal covered Jim's body.

At least they were all breathing.

"We need to get them to LexCorp," Hank said. The scientists there could help with the radiation effects. "There's a lab not far from Landing Site C. If we get to the road, we can hitch."

Terri sighed wearily. "I don't know if I'm strong enough," she said.

Hank felt horribly sick himself, deep down on a molecular level. "We don't have a choice," he said. "We're not going to die out here."

Hank quickly collected pieces of wreckage to make stretchers for the crew. It was surprisingly easy to put together strips of metal and sling cloth from their spacesuits. Strangely, the metal joints seemed to fuse together at his touch.

Soon, it was dusk, and the sun wasn't as hot. Hank and Terri dragged Jim and Steve on the stretchers for a long while until they spotted a road. With the help of a pick-up truck driver, they reached the LexCorp laboratory.

A heavy-set guard ran out to meet them as Terri and Hank pulled Jim and Steve from the truck's bed. Two other guards followed, both holding rifles.

"Help us!" Terri cried. "Please!"

"You can't be here," the guard said in alarm. "Leave now!"

"Call Lex Luthor," Hank said. "Please."

The guard whipped out a communicator. "Luthor," he said. "Front gate here. We have four paranormals in a pickup truck. Please advise."

Paranormals? Hank wondered. Then he realized why: Steve and Terri were glowing, Jim was covered in metal and stones, and Hank's hair had gone white. They looked like aliens. Or mutants.

"Paranormals aren't my problem," Lex Luthor replied clearly through the communicator. "Call Superman."

CHAPTER 3

EVOLUTION

"My name's Hank Henshaw," Hank told the guard. "I work for Luthor. We crashed in the desert after our space mission."

Suddenly, Terri screamed. Her skin was now glowing as bright as a laser beam. Hank caught her before she hit the pavement, but he was so weak he nearly toppled over.

The guard looked uncertainly at the people in front of him. Jim was coated in pieces of metal and rubble. Steve's body blazed with blue light. Terri and Hank looked deathly ill.

The guard bit his lip. "Okay," he told his men. "Let's get them into a medical lab – one we can quarantine. You inform Luthor, and I'll get in touch with Superman."

The guards carried *Excalibur*'s crew into the building. When the astronauts arrived in a medical lab with hospital beds and scientific equipment, the guards helped them onto the mattresses. One wall was lined with windows. Along the back wall was a hulking, tubular Magnetic Resonance Imaging machine – also known as a MRI – which used a magnetic field to examine the inside of a human body.

Hank slumped into his bed. He was exhausted, but filled with a strange energy that came from inside him. He glanced over at Terri. Her skin was transparent and red. He could almost see right through her.

"We'll be okay," Hank said to her.

"Hank," Terri moaned. "I . . . I feel like I'm falling apart."

Just then, Lex Luthor strode into the lab. "What are they doing here?" he demanded. "I specifically said they weren't my problem!"

"Sir," the head guard replied, "I couldn't leave them outside. They're terribly hurt. And they said they work for you. That one said his name is Hank Henshaw."

"Dr Henshaw?" Luthor said, peering at Hank. "What have you done to yourself? Are those others Terri and the astronauts?"

"Yes," Hank croaked. "We were hit by a solar flare. Then the shuttle crashed."

KNOCK! KNOCK! A noise came from the window. Superman hovered outside the lab.

The guard hurried over to let Superman in. "This had better be legal, Luthor," Superman said.

Lex raised his hands. "Everything's perfectly legal," he said. "These people were on the space shuttle *Excalibur* on a scientific mission. Their shuttle was hit by a solar flare. The radiation did something . . . interesting to their bodies."

Superman used his X-ray vision to peer inside their bodies. "Interesting?" Superman said. "It's killing them, Luthor. The radiation rearranged their atoms in ways I've never seen before. It's more than they can handle. We have to help them."

Hank could barely hear Superman's words. He groaned. He'd never experienced such pain before. But the strange part was that he'd never felt so . . . powerful.

Hank concentrated on the intense energy that was coursing through him. It helped to distract him from the pain.

When Hank looked at Terri, he saw that she was starting to vanish! It was like her body was passing into another dimension. She shimmered like pure energy.

"Terri, hold on," Hank said.

"Hank?" Terri whispered. She glanced around uncertainly. "Are you still there?"

"I'm here," Hank said. "I'm right here."

Suddenly, Steve sat up. He flared with purple energy . . . and then floated off the bed. "Too much!" he yelled. He began to spin in the air, glowing as brightly as a small sun. *FZZZZZZZZZZZT!* He streaked to the window, blasted through the glass, and zoomed outside into the sky.

Superman followed Steve into the atmosphere. Soon they were both out of Hank's sight.

THUMP! A noise made Hank look behind him. While Steve was flying off, Jim had been dragging his body, covered with metal and rocks, to the MRI machine. He crawled into the machine's tunnel.

"What does he think he's doing?" Luthor asked.

Jim shook his metal mess of a head. "I need to know what's wrong with me," he moaned. Jim raised a hand and clenched it into a fist. With it, he turned the MRI machine on.

"What are you doing?" Hank cried. "It'll kill you!"

With a heavy blink of his pebble-covered eyelids, Jim opened his hand. At least, it looked like a hand. His entire body was so completely covered in chunks of metal and stone that Hank couldn't see his skin.

The MRI machine's tube glowed with an electromagnetic field. Jim said something, but his voice sounded like metal being scraped by stone. Then the MRI's electromagnetism pulled at Jim's metal parts, ripping them off. With a gravelly shudder, the rocks fell to the ground around the MRI unit . . . and Jim was nowhere to be seen.

Is he . . . gone? Hank wondered. *Will that happen to me?*

But for some reason, Hank didn't think so. Yes, his body had changed, but he felt wildly alive.

"The solar flare wasn't random," Luthor told Hank and Terri. "You probably didn't know that Superman was battling the Eradicator, a Kryptonian artificial humanoid. It was all over the news, especially when Superman threw the Eradicator into the Sun. That's what caused the solar flare that hit your shuttle."

Hank's eyes went wide. He couldn't believe what he was hearing. Just then, Superman flew in through the broken window. "That's not the full story, Lex," he said. He put his hand on Hank's shoulder. "I followed your friend into space. I'm sorry, but he was too fast – I couldn't catch him before he . . . flew into the Sun."

Hank shook with pain and fury. The state he was in seemed to make the strange power within him stronger.

SLAP! Hank pushed away Superman's hand from his shoulder.

Superman triggered the solar flare, Hank realized. *It was Superman's fault. He killed Jim and Steve!*

Raw rage rampaged through Hank. The metal frame of the bed under Hank trembled. It took him a moment to realize that the force within him was causing the metal vibrations. Furious might swelled inside him.

"What can we do to save them?" asked Superman.

"Hmm," Luthor said. "I don't think there's anything we can do for Henshaw. I've never seen anything like this before. But the radiation is making his wife phase into another physical state."

"We could try to neutralize the solar radiation with a different frequency," Lex said. "The crew of *Excalibur* collected a sample of high-frequency radiation – that might work."

"Then do it," decided Superman.

"*You* do it," Luthor said. "I shouldn't even be in here now, near all this radiation. I'm getting behind a lead wall."

Their words made little sense to Hank. He was focusing on the energy welling up in him, along with the anger. It felt like this energy was trying to escape his body.

Then a realization struck Hank. *I feel trapped inside my body,* he thought.

The solution was simple. He needed to escape his weak, damaged body. It was scary, but it was necessary.

Maybe it would be like moving to a new form of existence. He probably wouldn't die. No, he was sure he wouldn't. He would transform into something else! He wasn't sure how he knew, but Hank felt convinced.

And Terri can join me, Hank thought. *Together, in our new, powerful forms.*

"Terri," Hank said. "I'm . . . changing. I can feel it. So are you."

Hank put his hand on her shoulder. Terri looked at him, seeing him now. "Let it happen," Hank said. "Come with me. It's a new stage of existence."

Terri nodded. Her head blazed with energy. "Like shedding . . . our skin?"

Hank nodded. "Exactly," he said. "You feel it too, don't you?"

Terri nodded. She closed her eyes.

Hank closed his eyes, too. He arched his back, and the energy inside him flowed out of his mouth. He suffered a moment of intense agony as he left his body behind.

Immediately, Hank felt free of the pain. *Am I still me?* he wondered. When he saw Superman helping Lex Luthor set up a radiation emitter near Terri's bed, he filled with anger again. *Yes,* he realized. *I still hate Superman. So I'm still me.*

But where was he? Hank concentrated on narrowing his attention. He realized his view started above a desk, with a chair in the way.

I'm inside a computer, Hank realized, *peering out of a webcam!*

Lex stepped away from Hank's body. "Henshaw is dead," he said to Superman.

"And his wife is going quickly," Lex said. "If you're going to do something, do it now." Luthor hurried out of the room.

With a shift of concentration, Hank swivelled the webcam to focus on Terri in her bed. Terri arched her back, preparing to release herself into her new form.

Don't be afraid, Hank thought.

A flash made Hank automatically swivel the webcam to the right. He saw Superman standing behind a tall radiation emitter, shooting a beam of blue radiance at Terri. Attached to the emitter was the canister of radiation that Hank had collected in space.

The Henshaw rays! Hank thought in panic. He struggled to free his consciousness from the webcam, to stop Superman from using the radiation on Terri, but he only wiggled the webcam weakly.

Terri was leaving her body. A ghostly red silhouette floated out of her mouth. Superman turned a dial on the emitter, and the beam shined brighter.

ZRRRRRRRRT! Terri's energy sank back into her body. The Henshaw rays were working. The red radioactive glow dimmed on her skin. Her colour returned to normal.

Tears streamed from Terri's eyes. "Hank!" she cried out. "I tried, Hank! Where are you, Hank?"

Superman had saved Terri's life.

But Hank knew that Terri was now locked in her body for as long as she lived. She would never be able to join him now.

Hank let out a furious scream. But no one could hear him.

CHAPTER 4

GHOST IN THE MACHINE

Hank thrashed around inside the webcam. He couldn't do anything about Superman saving Terri.

Then he realized something. *I am pure energy now,* he thought. *I'm not trapped anywhere!*

He didn't have to stay inside the webcam. The connected computer was powered up, so he could follow the webcam's USB cord into the computer itself. It wasn't dark inside the computer as Hank had expected. Instead, the circuits inside had their own glow.

With a little effort, Hank found that he could travel through the computer's memory as if he was walking along the streets of a huge high-tech city! The wires, chips, cards and other technological components inside the computer thrummed with energy as if they were alive.

It was a medical lab computer, so all the information stored on the hard drive was about various drugs LexCorp was developing. None of it was particularly interesting to Hank – he was a physicist, not a pharmacologist.

After expanding his power to explore more of the computer's workings, Hank followed the electronic pathways that led through the wires to the LexCorp mainframe. He got stuck for a moment with the password authentication.

But when Hank concentrated, the technology bowed to his will and he gained access. He slipped inside the interconnected computer network for the whole of LexCorp.

So much information, Hank thought, in awe. With a little bit of focus, he could access any electronic area of LexCorp. He opened himself up to all the knowledge a genius such as Luthor collected.

Information rushed through him in a flood of digital bits. He could access the weapons technology LexCorp was researching, all of its property deals and all of Luthor's devious plans for achieving world domination. He drank it all in, and felt his power grow by leaps and bounds.

Knowledge is power, he thought. *And I want it all!*

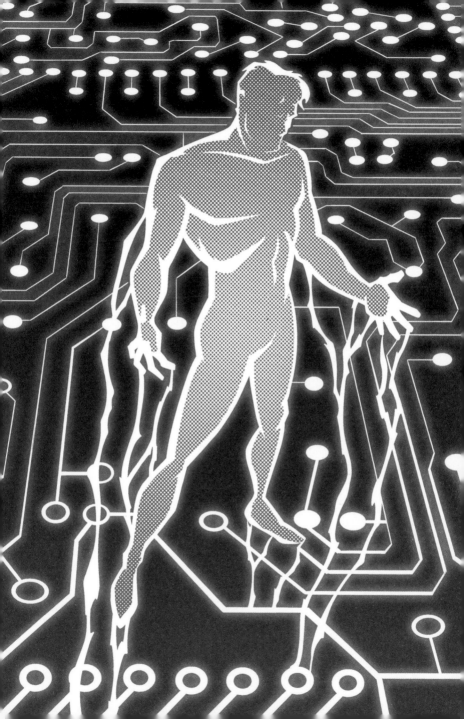

Hank found his own file in LexCorp's personnel records. He inspected the reports on his mission to outer space. Then he saw his personal bio. Under his picture, in red type, was the word *DECEASED*.

Sorrow rippled through Hank. As much as he was grateful that his consciousness lived on, it was hard to face the fact that his body had died. He was now an electronic ghost. That idea overwhelmed him, and he lost control of the information flow he was absorbing. The mass of data overwhelmed his mind, and Hank lost track of who he was in the torrent.

Hank blacked out. By the time his subconscious came back into focus, days had passed. Hank was still whirling about in a waterfall of data, and he felt frighteningly fragile.

He reached out to the circuits of the computer, and found a buffer switch. With a thrust of power, Hank pressed the soldered metal circuit, applying all the force he could. *CLICK!* The buffer switch flipped, and the raging river of information slowed to a trickle.

How did I do that? Hank wondered. He inspected the tiny soldered circuit, and made an incredible discovery. He could see the molecular patterns in the metal, down to the atoms that made up the circuit's matter!

Not only did Hank know how to inhabit technology – to live inside it – but he could also make it move. Right now he could only manipulate the tiniest man-made objects. But he would grow stronger with practice. He knew it.

Hank checked the LexCorp database for any news about Terri. Her vital signs were stable, but she had been moved to a space research facility near Metropolis.

Although Hank wanted to travel through the wires and networks so he could immediately be by her side, he didn't yet have the power to travel such a large distance. First he needed to harness, and learn to control, his strength.

Hank realized he could see Terri by accessing the security cameras at the research facility. He found a low-resolution video feed of her in a small, cosy room on a high floor. Terri slumped in her bed, barely moving. She looked terribly sad.

It was all Superman's fault. Hank could have been with his wife forever, sharing in the power of a new existence.

But Superman ruined all that by saving Terri's life. No, just her *body*.

Hank would make Superman pay.

For days, Hank honed his skills. He stretched and strengthened his mental muscles, learning how to manipulate machinery and control technology. Hank called this power *technomorphing* – changing technology. He could move and operate and morph together screws and gears, wires and sockets, microchips and electronic circuitry.

A few days later, Hank had moved on from manipulating basic machinery to controlling complex equipment such as lasers, the trucks in the parking area, the forklift and the entire electrical and communications system of the facility.

Finally, the entire computer network and all the technology in LexCorp was under his control. He hid any sign of his influence from the doctors and scientists – and certainly from Lex Luthor himself.

Once Hank felt that his skills were strong enough, he prepared to transfer his consciousness to the facility where Terri was being held. Hank compressed himself into as small a data packet as he could, and released whatever useless information he had gathered.

Hank reached out through all the broadband networks that linked to LexCorp, and cleared as much bandwidth for his use as possible. Then he said goodbye to the safety of the lab's mainframe, and he launched himself into the internet.

It was a whirling, dizzying roller coaster of a ride, zipping along the information highway at the speed of electricity. He followed routers and servers and ricocheted through computer equipment, making sure all of himself passed smoothly to each jumping point.

Finally he reached the computer server for the research facility. Hank easily bypassed security by tweaking their hardware, then he slipped inside the mainframe. He absorbed all their stored information. Most of it was rocket science data, much of which he had already learned as a scientist. But there were also files about secret government and military projects.

With his new knowledge, Hank could launch thousands of missiles and destroy Earth.

But he didn't want to destroy Earth. He wanted to kill Superman.

First, though, Hank had to rescue Terri.

Hank saw that she was kept in a bare room on the fourteenth floor where doctors regularly performed tests on her. Hank waited until the floor was mostly empty. Then he moved his consciousness to a cluttered computer server room near by.

He used the metal plates, processors, circuitry and wiring of the servers to pull together a gleaming, mobile skeleton. For his skull, he attached a server box to a speaker so that he could talk, a microphone to hear and two webcams for eyes. He embedded a WiFi server in his chest so he could stay connected to the electronic realm.

It was the most impressive technological body he could create with what was available to him, and Hank was pleased with how smoothly it moved. The skeletal structure bristled with wires and circuits, shimmering with the intense power of Hank's energy force.

CLUNK! CLANK! CLUNK! Hank left the server room and clunked down the corridor towards his wife's room. He opened her door and stepped inside.

Terri was sitting on the edge of her bed, staring out of the window into the darkness. Then Terri's eyes flicked up, and she saw his reflection in the window . . . and let out a scream. **AHHHHHHHHHHHHH!**

"No, no, Terri," Hank rasped, raising his metal claws to show that he was harmless. "Terri, calm down!"

"A monster!" Terri shrieked.

"No, it's me, Hank!" he said. "I'm in a better body now. Listen to my voice!"

Terri shook her head. "You're a fake," she said flatly. "Hank is dead."

"I'm not dead," Hank replied. "I'm just improved –"

"Hank's dead!" Terri cried. She jumped to her feet and backed away.

Hank moved towards her with his arms outstretched. "Terri," he said, trying to speak softly, but his voice was a mechanical screech. "Please, believe that it's me!"

Terri lurched back, away from Hank until she hit the window. **CRASH!** The glass shattered. Before Hank could react, Terri fell gracefully through the smashed window and into the dark night beyond.

CHAPTER 5

CYBORG SUPERMAN

Hank didn't need to look out of the window. He knew there was no way that Terri could have survived the fourteen-storey fall.

Although his technological body couldn't feel emotions, his inner core, his energy, was devastated. Terri had been his wife and friend. Without her, Hank had no one left to love.

But he did have one person left to hate.

"It's all Superman's fault," Hank croaked. Superman had caused the solar flare when he threw the Eradicator into the Sun. He had trapped Terri in her human form with the Henshaw rays, separating her energy from Hank's.

Hank's fury shook the foundations of the research facility. The lights flickered, overpowering the building's systems with his rage.

Connected wirelessly to the facility's network, Hank used the energy of his anger to fuel a worldwide search for data. Somewhere on Earth there must be information on how to kill Superman.

While back at LexCorp, Hank had learned about Kryptonite, and about all of Luthor's failed attempts to destroy Superman.

Kryptonite wasn't enough – Superman's multi-levelled powers were so tricky that merely weakening him had proven ineffective.

And now, searching the world's electronic archives, Hank found nothing but records of botched efforts to kill the Man of Steel. Superman was invulnerable. Indestructible.

But that was impossible. Superman was alive, and so the opposite must be true – there must be a way to destroy him. If that information wasn't on Earth, then Hank would leave the planet and find the trick to destroying the Man of Steel in another universe.

How do I leave Earth, though? Hank wondered. *Humans have only managed flights within our small solar system.*

There was one alien on the planet who was capable of interstellar travel. Superman himself. But Superman's secrets weren't on Earth's information grid. He must store them somewhere, in some kind of hideout. *Where does Superman live?* Hank asked himself.

Dropping his mechanical body, Hank scanned the web of electricity that blanketed the world. It was a complete grid, criss-crossing the land and much of the oceans. Hank checked for a blank spot, somewhere that wasn't connected to the grid. His search strained the planet's electrical system, causing power cuts across the planet. But finally he noticed a tiny blank spot.

In the Arctic, near the North Pole, he found a self-contained place.

The place was powered by alien energy and was connected to Earth's information grid, but only one-way. That meant that information went into the blank spot, but nothing came out.

There it is, Hank thought.

Hank sent himself through the grid, speeding towards the energy gap near the North Pole.

Upon arrival, Hank tried to enter the area, but he smacked up against technology he didn't understand. It was alien in design, formed with other-worldly crystals carrying electrical impulses. The structure was advanced beyond anything created by humans.

At first, Hank was baffled by the strange workings of Superman's hideout.

He lurked along the edge of the information grid, trying to work out how to penetrate the alien structure. He had to hurry – his powerful consciousness strained the world's grid. Soon the whole system would fizzle.

Yes, it's alien, Hank thought, *but it's still technology. I can control technology.*

Hank noticed that the energy surging through the crystals was solar energy – it was powered by Earth's yellow star. The Sun. Hank realized that a solar flare had given him his technomorphing power. *If there's one thing I know now,* Hank thought, *it's our Sun!*

He increased his energy up to the highest solar radiation frequencies he could manage, up to Henshaw rays . . . and beyond!

Soon, Hank was vibrating in a spectrum he hadn't known existed.

DING! And just like that, Hank was granted access.

Hank slipped inside the structure. He was bombarded by a torrent of alien information. He struggled to process it. The bizarre frequencies were so surprising, and the crystal technology was so intricate, that Hank almost lost himself.

But he would have his revenge on Superman. He would avenge Terri.

Hank's technomorphing power revved so hot, he worried it would short-circuit his consciousness. But he began to understand how the alien technology worked.

It was strange and marvellous and like nothing Hank had ever experienced.

The designers had used technology that was far more advanced than Earth's capabilities. If he worked out how the crystals carried the information in their complex structures, he could access the data itself. Hank began to absorb what Superman knew.

Superman was an alien from a destroyed planet called Krypton. His Kryptonian name was Kal-El. He, too, was powered by the energy of the yellow Sun, which gave him his amazing abilities. The crystal building near the North Pole was called the Fortress of Solitude. Superman had crash-landed on Earth as a child, and was raised by humans, the Kents, in Smallville, Kansas. In fact, the surviving pieces of Kal-El's spaceship formed the core of the Fortress of Solitude.

All the knowledge of Krypton's ancient, destroyed civilization was contained in the crystals of the Kryptonian Matrix Cluster at the centre of the Fortress. The crystals held all the information available about Superman, too, down to a full map of his DNA.

Hank downloaded all the incredible alien information into himself hungrily. Superman was awesomely powerful, with few weaknesses. No human could challenge him and survive.

To destroy Superman, Hank realized, *I need to become Superman.*

With his technomorphing power, the Kryptonian technology and Superman's DNA, Hank built a new body for himself – one that mixed the best of machinery and Superman's powerful form.

Hank knew how to clone Superman's flesh, and graft it onto mighty metallic parts he found in the Fortress of Solitude. He made a body that was better than Superman's, because he could morph the technology into any weapon he wanted.

Hank had just finished creating his new body when Superman arrived.

THUMP! Superman landed a couple of metres away from Hank inside the Fortress. "I don't know who you are," Superman said, "but you have stolen from me. You are not welcome here."

"I've taken what's yours," Hank replied, "because you took everything I had. You destroyed my human existence. And you killed my wife."

"Wife?" Superman asked. "Henshaw, is that you? What have you done to yourself?"

Hank's reply was to raise his metallic arm. It was equipped with a laser rifle. He shot a blast at Superman, aiming for his head.

Superman leaped into the air, dodging the attack. "Fighting me is not going to change anything," he said.

ZRRRRRRRRRT! Superman fried Hank's laser cannon with a burst of his heat vision.

Hank laughed. "I can do anything you can do!" he said. He slowly raised himself into the air. Then he shot back his own beam of heat vision.

ZAP!

Superman soared out of the way of the blast, then circled around to face Hank again. "Hank," he said, "I didn't kill your wife. I saved her life."

"You stopped her from joining me!" Hank's voice box crackled. "We would have been united in a universe of infinite power. You stole her from me forever!"

Hank launched himself at Superman, planning to hit him with his hardest punch. But Superman sidestepped Hank in the air.

KA-THUD!

Superman hammered both hands onto Hank's back, knocking him off-balance. Hank spun down, crashing into the middle of the Fortress.

"You may have my powers," Superman said, "but you don't have my experience or skill. There are things you cannot learn from information alone."

He'll beat me, Hank realized. *He's been training as a super hero his whole life. I'm like a white belt in karate attacking a black belt.*

"Give yourself up," Superman said. "I will work with you and help you adapt to your new body. Learn how to use it responsibly. It's the only thing that will save your life now, Hank."

"Like you saved Terri?" Hank squawked. "I don't need your kind of help!"

But he knew Superman was right. Hank couldn't stay in the Fortress of Solitude. He couldn't beat Superman.

Yet.

There was a whole universe to explore, a nearly infinite expanse to discover. He could add new powers and new abilities, adapt to unknown alien technologies and gain experience to grow a million times stronger.

Hank lurched over to the Kryptonian Matrix Cluster, and collapsed on top of it. He absorbed the technological core of Kal-El's original interstellar ship into his body. Then he combined with it to become a creature that could travel through space.

"Don't run!" Superman said. "Stay, and we'll help you together!"

He's lying, Hank thought. *He's just afraid of what I'll become. And he should be afraid.*

Hank blasted up from the base of the Fortress of Solitude, crashed through the crystal roof, and soared into open air.

At super-speed, Superman donned his spacesuit, then gave chase. He followed Hank up through the atmosphere.

"Henshaw!" Superman shouted. "I apologize for the way this has turned out. Come back, and we'll find a way to help you!"

Lies, Hank thought. *All lies.* Superman's words enraged him, and filled him with more energy. He zoomed off Earth, past where *Excalibur* had flown, and headed towards Mars.

Superman stayed close on his tail past Mars, but by the time Hank neared Jupiter, Superman started to fall behind.

Hank had Superman's ability of spaceflight, but he also had the additional power of his Kryptonian spaceship built right into his body. Meanwhile, the yellow light of Earth's Sun was growing weaker, and therefore so were Superman's powers.

Hank lost Superman just past Jupiter. Then Hank headed towards Saturn, and the infinite universe beyond.

The exhilaration of limitless possibilities flooded Hank as he rocketed through space. He would discover endless alien worlds. He would learn things that other humans wouldn't even dream.

But he would never forget that he had a mission to accomplish. *I will grow strong with alien technologies and experience,* Hank thought. *I will become inhumanly powerful.*

And when I return, Hank thought, *I'll be the mightiest cyborg in the universe.*

He would design himself specifically to destroy Kal-El from Krypton. He would take his name, his home planet and then his life.

"I am Cyborg Superman," Hank said as he zoomed past Neptune and out into the unknown.

CYBORG SUPERMAN

Real Name:
Hank Henshaw

Occupation:
Former astronaut

Base:
Unknown

Height:
Varies

Weight:
Varies

Eyes:
Blue

Hair:
Black

Having interacted with devices in Superman's Fortress of Solitude, Hank Henshaw gained the knowledge of Kryptonian technology. This information allows him to bond flesh and metal however he pleases. The process also gives him a variety of superpowers, some of which are unique. He is now known as Cyborg Superman, or simply the Cyborg.

- Cyborg Superman has all of Superman's superpowers. He also has the ability to control and absorb all forms of machinery and technology.

- He also has an ability called technopathy, which allows him to interact mentally with computers, the internet and anything digital.

- Using a power called technokinesis, Cyborg Superman can move electronics by simply using his mind.

BIOGRAPHIES

J. E. BRIGHT has had more than 50 novels, novelizations and non-fiction books published for children and young adults. He is a full-time freelance writer, living in a tiny apartment in New York, USA, with his good, fat cat, Gladys, and his evil cat, Mabel, who is getting fatter.

TIM LEVINS is best known for his work on the Eisner Award-winning DC Comics series, Batman: Gotham Adventures. Tim has illustrated other DC titles, such as Justice League Adventures, Batgirl, Metal Men and Scooby Doo, and has also done work for Marvel Comics and Archie Comics. Tim enjoys life in Ontario, Canada, with his wife, son, puppy and two horses.

GLOSSARY

agonizing unbearable or miserable

atmosphere mixture of gases that surrounds a planet

consciousness thoughts or feelings of an individual

DNA molecule that carries the genetic code that gives living things their special characteristics. The letters stand for DeoxyriboNucleic Acid.

electromagnetism magnetic effect that occurs when electricity flows through a coil of wire

exosphere highest region of the atmosphere

g-force force acting on a body as a result of acceleration or gravity

intricate detailed and complicated

radiation rays of light, heat or particles that are sent out from a radioactive substance

radioactive giving off harmful radiation

DISCUSSION QUESTIONS

1. Who is more of a villain in this book – Lex Luthor or Cyborg Superman? Discuss your answer.

2. Do you think it was fair for Hank Henshaw to blame Superman for his wife's death? Why or why not?

3. This book has ten illustrations. Which one is your favourite? Why?

WRITING PROMPTS

1. Explain why you think Cyborg Superman wants revenge on the Man of Steel. Use specific examples from the story to support your claim.

2. Recreate yourself as a cyborg! Firstly, write a paragraph about your new, robotic appearance. Secondly, write a paragraph about what you'd do with your new powers. Finally, draw a picture of your cyborg self.

3. Imagine that Cyborg Superman returns to Earth. What does he do? How does Superman defeat a mechanical version of himself? Write about it.